Pat,

With all best wishes

from

Bunch –

CHILDREN OF THE SUN-GOD

CHILDREN OF THE SUN-GOD

Diana Macgregor

The Book Guild Ltd
Sussex, England

Although they were real people, Montezuma, the Aztec Emperor, and Cortes, the Spanish Commander, are depicted in an imaginary fashion. All other characters are fictional.

The Book Guild Ltd.
25 High Street,
Lewes, Sussex

First published 1999
© Diana Macgregor

Set in Baskerville
Typesetting by
Acorn Bookwork, Salisbury, Wiltshire
Printed in Great Britain by
Bookcraft (Bath) Ltd, Avon

A catalogue record for this book is
available from the British Library

ISBN 1 85776 461 7

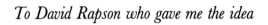

To David Rapson who gave me the idea

CONTENTS

Isaac spake unto Abraham his father, and said, 'My father –
where is the lamb for a burnt offering?'
And Abraham said, 'God will provide Himself the lamb for a
burnt offering, my son.'
And Abraham bound Isaac his son and laid him on the altar,
and took out a knife to slay his son. And the angel of the Lord
called to him out of heaven, and said, 'Abraham, Abraham.'
And he said, 'Here am I.'
And he said, 'Lay not thy hand upon the lad, neither do thou
anything to him.'

–Genesis, Chapter 22, vv. 7–12. Revised Standard Version

AUTHOR'S NOTE

The characters in this story are fictitious, apart from Montezuma, the Aztec emperor, and Cortés, who was the Spanish
commander.

The events took place in the sixteenth century. The Aztec
empire covered roughly the area now called Mexico.

The Aztec pyramids, unlike those of Ancient Egypt which
were smooth-sided, were built in a series of platforms. In the
centre of the sides, steps were cut.

1

The High Priest of the Sun-God

'Are the victims ready for sacrificing?'

'Yes, Your Excellency ... yes ... but ...' the Chief Temple Priest faltered and became silent. The High Priest threw him a look that was sharply haughty.

'They are. Then why are you making difficulties?'

Inside the temple buildings the rooms were dusky and cool. Outside, the brilliant rays of the Mexican sun beat fierce hammer blows on the stone buildings of the Aztec capital.

The other still hesitated. Why had he appointed a man who so irritated him? At last the answer came, flustered yet obsequious.

'As, of course, Your Excellency knows ... more victims would be desirable ... it's ... the people ... they are uneasy.'

The High Priest threw him a hard, disdainful look.

'I'm fully aware of that,' he rapped arrogantly. 'The present campaign should provide enough prisoners for the festival. Their blood will be sufficient to strengthen our mighty god, the sun.'

After that he remained in a silence of contempt. The audience was at an end. Rebuffed, the Chief Temple Priest bowed and withdrew. His superior stared hard after him.

'Making needless difficulties as usual,' he summed up caustically.

As if he were not perfectly aware of the situation. For a decade past there had been disturbing signs and portents. A baby with two heads had been born. Then, Popocatepetl had

1

suddenly awaked from its long slumber, flinging smoke and fire to the heavens and spewing seas of boiling lava over the countryside. Now there was this frightening comet, trailing a tail of flames across the sky. No wonder the people were alarmed and upset and the priests troubled with bad dreams.

Not even His Imperial Majesty, the great Montezuma, the 'Courageous Lord' himself, was free from fearsome forebodings.

His mind went back to his last audience with the Emperor. It had followed the usual unsatisfactory course. He had found him poring over the ancient texts. Of course, His Imperial Majesty ought to study the scriptures ... but ...

Approaching him, he had made the three bows and recited the words, 'Lord, my Lord, my great Lord', that etiquette demanded.

Montezuma had motioned him to be seated, a privilege that he alone enjoyed.

'The signs and prophesies all point to it.'

'Yes, Your Imperial Majesty.'

'Before long, the white god will return to our land,' and Montezuma had raised dark, troubled eyes to him for a moment.

He had lowered his own, of course; no one looked the Emperor in the face. So he was still obsessed with the idea that the god of wind and life, the Feathered Serpent, was coming back to them.

'As he promised us he would, before he left us, millenia ago.' The words chimed in on his thoughts.

'You are convinced that our scriptures foretell it, Your Imperial Majesty?'

'They do. It will be a time of great trial and tribulation for our people.'

He had paused tactfully, then said deferentially, 'Perhaps if I might suggest, Your Imperial Majesty?' Again the dark, deeply anxious eyes had scanned his face, but did not forbid his speaking. 'Your Imperial Majesty, whatever the prophecies may say, I feel that we enjoy the favour of the gods, as your victories in battle clearly testify. It cannot be impossible for us to win the favour of Quetzalcoatl, the god of wind and life too, should he come.'

Montezuma had studied him for a long time with grave thoughtfulness. At length his reply came heavily, earnestly, but it was far from encouraging.

'Let us hope that you are right.'

On this depressing, uncertain note the audience had ended.

The stream of sacrificial victims, prisoners from the battle-field, and levies from the conquered tribes, had swollen to a flood. Appeased, gratified, gorged, the gods would surely continue to smile upon their worshippers.

But for all his words the High Priest felt uneasy. No one knew how to propitiate him ... For the god of wind and life, the Feathered Serpent, disapproved of human sacrifice.

2

The Sun Must Shine

Masked, white-robed, he stood on the topmost stage of the lofty pyramid, long quartz knife in hand. It dripped blood. The altar was already streaming blood. High over him towered the hideously masked idols of the war gods: the god of the sun and the god of darkness and evil.

The next victim was escorted up the steps by four priests, chanting a weird dirge. He struggled violently, uselessly. They tied him down. Agony was on his face. A crimson gash split the chest open. The rhythmic drumbeats rose, but failed to drown his screaming.

A deadly pause: he raised the blood-smeared knife. A swift, skilled cut, a twist, and he ripped out the still beating heart and tossed it into the sacred casket. Held aloft, it was offered to the idols, then tipped onto the wet, slippery pile. Of no further use, the body was kicked down the steps, to roll into the blood-soaked mêlée below.

It had begun at dawn. Now the rays of the noonday sun hammered fiercely upon the reddening stones of the pyramid and the blood-drenched altar. They beat savagely onto the exulting High priest and his white-robed, masked assistants and the tense, unnaturally excited crowd that watched in fascination from the square below.

Next came a man of high rank, an Eagle Knight, who sought glorious immortality by offering his life. Painted white and wearing a crown of waving feathers, he walked boldly up the steps, accompanied by the chanting priests. He laid himself on the altar, and suffered the opening slash without a cry. The old soldier murmured a prayer to the god of darkness and evil. The drums beat louder and louder. The High Priest raised the long, stone, sacrificial knife. The drums crescendoed to a frenzy of sound. A stab and twist. Blood spurted like a fountain. The High Priest tore out the heart as it still beat. It was offered up to the gods. The soldier's soul was now winging its way to heaven; the corpse could be rolled down the steps to snare up in the gory, tangled heap beneath.

Excited, inflamed, the crowd was shouting and chanting hysterically in time with the drumbeats. Guarded by soldiers, the prisoners waited in an apathetic, terrified huddle. One by one they were seized and thrust forward into the hands of the priests, tied down and slaughtered.

It went on all day. The pyramid steps became slippery with blood. Blood dried on the paving stones of the city square. It spattered the robes of the priests and lay in pools boiling in the heat of the midday sun. It stuck to the High Priest's fingers and matted his hair. It covered the hands of his assistants, streamed off the altar and dripped down the pyramid steps. The ritual went on relentlessly as victim after victim was despatched.

The sun sank to a crimson horizon. The slaughter ceased. The crowd slowly drifted away, gorged with the sight of blood. Darkness fell; a horrible, empty silence stilled the feverish tumult.

It was over. The dead bodies lay in oozing, trickling piles; a mass of dripping hearts bulged in a soft, squelching mountain.

Spent, drained, but the High Priest knew that now the gods would have enough human blood to drink, enough human hearts to eat. Strengthened and given fresh life, the sun would rise in splendour each day and shine forth in all his power upon the earth. The harvest would be plentiful. Mankind was safe.

3

The Perfect Jewel Lady

He sat alone struggling with temple business. For a moment he let his thoughts drift to the Perfect Jewel Lady. How beautiful, how exquisite she was. Did she really love him? He tried to attend to tedious, mundane matters once more. But despite his efforts, she filled his mind ... her flashing eyes, dainty, little hands, enticing breasts. He longed for her, only to be with her, to say a few words to her. But was it true that she had been seeing the Jaguar Prince again? The thought twisted in his mind, tormented him. That hateful man was high-born, a commander; but that was no reason for her dallying with him. She must realise that he, the High Priest, was a far better man. How he longed to see the fellow dead.

Outside, the city scorched in furnace-like heat. The rays of the noonday sun spared nothing; its blows struck huts and stone buildings alike and smote the gigantic pyramid, drying up the blood splashed on it. Even the bustle and hum of the nearby market were stifled and stilled.

Within the cool building the priests went softly to and fro about their business. But the heart of the High Priest knew no stillness, no peace. It burned with jealousy, boiled in lust. Even the volcano, Popocatepetl, could not have spewed forth such a deadly stream of raging, red-hot hatred.

* * * * * *

The litter of the Jaguar Prince jerked to a halt and the

commander sprang eagerly from it. There was but one thought in his mind: would she deign to see him?

The large brick house stood alone, its outlines as sharp as flint edges in the piercing rays of the sun. The ugly, oblong shadow it threw was as black as night. On all sides cultivated land stretched to the horizon; on this her slaves sweated, preparing the rich soil, bent double as they toiled in the murderous heat. The landscape seemed crawling with them.

But the Prince did not throw a glance in their direction. He strode swiftly under the archway and across the courtyard. The stifling heat bouncing back from brick walls and rising from flagged paving stones, wrapped him around like a hot, thick, heavy cloak.

The dusky little maidservant had been on the outlook for him, it seemed.

Eyes smiling mischievously, she greeted him with the faintest dip and 'Yes, Your Honour, I will certainly tell the mistress that you have come,' and off she tiptoed, barefoot and giggling.

The main room was large, spacious and cool. His heart leapt when he saw her. The beautiful young widow reclined gracefully on a couch-like rug. Her colouring was lightly brown. Dark eyes flashed like liquid fire in a neat, oval face that had dainty features and perfectly even, white teeth. Her limbs were delicately long and slender and her waist, slim and tiny. She wore a tunic and skirt of the sheerest pale blue cotton, bordered with colourfully flowered embroidery. The ends of her black hair, piled in conventional horn-shaped fashion on the top of her head, were glossy and saucy. Her dainty wrists were encircled by elegant gold bracelets and her slender neck adorned by a finely twisted rope of gold. Although pretending indifference, as the squat, strongly-built man came in, her eyes gave a flash of delight at seeing him. As she rose she showed her tiny feet in their gold-thonged slippers and a pair of shapely ankles ... enough to be enticing.

The little maid had disappeared. They were alone.

'My Perfect Jewel Lady, how beautiful you are.'

She smiled entrancingly, and held out her dainty, little hands to him.

'How wonderful to see you again, my brave Jaguar Prince.'

But did she know what he had come to see her about? She led him to the rug couch. Casting aside his rich jaguar skin cloak, he settled himself there. Her welcome was far warmer than he had dared to hope, but he had a painful matter to discuss with her. He bided his time. Chocolate drinks were brought and he noticed that she smiled softly as she drank hers. What was she thinking?

When they were alone once more, she turned to him and seemed to be waiting for him to speak. He must make the first move.

'It's lovely to see you again,' he began, hesitated, and then came straight to the point. 'But is it true, what I hear ... that he's been seeing you?'

Her eyes gave a flicker, but he could not read her expression. 'Really,' she thought, 'how blunt he is. That's because he's a soldier, I don't doubt, very forthright.' But her only reply was a mysterious smile. He was irritated.

'Why don't you answer me?'

'Mother always said that girls shouldn't be heard to speak,' she replied mischievously.

'Your mother was too strict with you. Besides, it's a bit different now, you're grown up and a widow and, anyway, it's only the two of us talking together. Do tell me,' he wheedled, 'is it true?'

'I do believe you're jealous of him,' she teased. 'But don't let's talk about that. Now you're here, tell me something nice.'

Really she was impossible. What could a man do? There was a pause while he tried to think what to say.

'Your eyes are as lovely as Metzliapan, the Moon Lake,' he managed. This brought a flashing smile to her face and she moved her slender, dainty hands, setting the gold bracelets chinking softly. So far so good. But she had still not given him an answer. He tried again. 'You are as beautiful as a hibiscus flower, as divine as a goddess.'

'Flatterer.'

'No, I mean every word of it.'

But still she gave no answer to his question.

* * * * * *

'How long can you stay?' she asked.

The sun was beginning its downward curve; the unbearable heat was easing. Well, she had not asked him to stay longer so he must think carefully.

'Not as long as I'd like.' Then he put on his brisk, military manner. 'I've been invited to the banquet given by His Imperial Majesty ... can't very well refuse.'

Her eyebrows rose.

'No, you can't do that. Isn't it rather unusual, though, for him to dine in public?'

'It is, most. But it's a special occasion, the anniversary of his accession, also of his great victory. All the high-ups are going.'

'I must not keep you away from it.'

'No, but I'd far rather be with you.'

She gave him a sparkling smile.

There was a pause and then he said, 'I've brought you a little something.'

'Have you really? It's too kind of you.'

He was aware of her interest as, with a languid movement she took the tiny box that he handed to her and gently, slowly laid back the carved lid. There it lay, cushioned on a bed of seeds: an ornament of polished green jade, shaped like a fish. Her eyes lit up.

'But it's lovely.'

'It's as perfect as you are. Put it on.'

She did so, placing the slender gold cord around her neck gracefully, so that the fish hung between her breasts.

9

'You are very generous, Coatl.'

'Not at all, darling. I love you.'

'Do you really?'

'Of course I do.'

But he dared not ask her if she loved him. There was a long, breathless, silence while he tried to make out her thoughts.

'Too bad you must go so soon. You must come and see me again before long.'

'Of course, I will. As soon as I can get away.'

Shortly after that he took his leave. Her smile as they parted mystified him.

4

The Banquet

The High Priest looked along the table. From his position at the end he had a perfect view; at the head was seated His Imperial Majesty, the Emperor, Montezuma himself. The hundred and more guests still standing lined the two sides, the priests of the sun-god on his right hand, those of the god of darkness and evil together with those of the god of wind and life, on his left. Next to these were placed the military commanders, men fierce and proud; with a stab of hatred he saw the Jaguar Prince among these of royal blood. Below them came the judges and foremost officials, then those of lesser degree. He, himself, held the place of honour – the only person able to look straight at the Emperor.

The dining hall of the gigantic stone palace was crowded, the hum of conversation and clatter of plates and bowls were hushed out of respect. The guests, all men, had laid aside their shoes and rich, feathered cloaks in the imperial presence. With a superior smirk he noticed their flower-bestitched loincloths, gaudily embroidered tunics and overmuch gold jewellery, all in contrast to his own black robes.

But if the guests were glittering, Montezuma outshone them all. He wore his most magnificent, finely embroidered tunic and cloak, a headdress of gold-studded peacock feathers the size of a cartwheel, and round his neck hung a heavy link chain of gold, which clasped an outsized jade jewel. Graciously condescending, he led the conversation with confidence; his hearers listened in polite silence, or ventured to agree, their faces turned away deferentially.

They ate huge quantities of turkey and pheasant with maize; the empty dishes were cleared away soundlessly, skilfully, by an army of barefoot servants. The sound of talking rose slowly, cautiously.

The High Priest looked around at the immense, spacious hall with its lofty ceiling, the supports decorated with heavy, circular scrollwork, and at the many-coloured, tessellated stone floor that was bare and cold underfoot. It was not the first time he had been to the palace, far from it, but it was the first time he had dined in the great hall. Further off, intricately carved furniture of wood and a glitter of elaborate gold ornaments caught his eye. Montezuma was, without doubt, the richest and most powerful ruler in the world. 'The Courageous Lord's' victories had increased his empire to a size never before known. Tribute came to him from countless conquered peoples; gold poured into his treasury from the mines. All this was due to his Imperial Majesty's being a devotee of the sun-god, of course.

Now for the venison and wild duck, along with green peppers and spicy tomato sauce. The Emperor was serviced first by four beautiful girls, who waited on him daintily, gracefully, with downcast eyes. There was a polite pause, then the guests began eating their portions. Next, pigeons and hares mixed with squashes arrived, truly delicious, especially after the long weeks of fasting before the last festival. Then came the final treat, the chocolate drinks, taken after the Emperor had finished his. One and all were satisfied. The sound of voices swelled once more, slowly, shyly at first, then more stridently. He permitted himself the briefest glance at the Emperor. His expression was hard to read for Montezuma, his dark inner thoughts well hidden, appeared sanguine and radiating good humour.

They had presented their gifts to him earlier. Skins of leopards and jaguars showered down like heavy rain. There were valuables heaped high, jewels of jade and ornaments of gold, wrought into a thousand curved animal, flower and scroll shapes. Men vied with one another for the honour of giving the most extravagant gift. Montezuma himself had shown a seemly mixture of indifference and gratitude; but his Chief Treasurer was of another ilk. The loathsome, suave timeserver with his oily manner and pettifogging ways, had, withal, the eyes of a hawk and a memory that was preposterous in its accuracy. No, it did not do to disappoint him. However, his gift of a calendar, a giant circular plate of solid gold, should prove acceptable and the temple coffers could easily stand the strain.

The 'Falling Eagle Prince' made a motion with his hand. The room fell silent. Obedient to custom, he delivered his speech without looking the Emperor in the face. The High Priest hid a sardonic look: for all his lack of intelligence, the fellow was close to the throne and a successful general. The boredom must be endured. He began.

'Your most mighty Imperial Majesty, we one and all wish, on this auspicious occasion, to congratulate Your Imperial Highness on the success of your reign, success that shines brightly even like our god, the sun, to applaud you on your never-ending victories, to praise your great wealth and power, your esteem among all peoples of the world and to express the honour and high respect in which your own people rightly hold you. We wish to thank you for the many years of prosperity that we, your subjects, have enjoyed since your most welcome accession to the throne of our land. We humbly wish Your Imperial Majesty countless more victories, many more years of wealth and happiness, and may the favour of the gods ever rest upon you for the remainder of a long and glorious reign.'

A subdued, respectful murmur of assent was heard. He glanced round. The approval was heartfelt. But had they known what he knew of Montezuma's inner mind, would they have felt so confident?

A discreet pause followed. Then the Emperor replied but in a fashion unexpectedly hesitant.

'We thank you from our heart for ... your words ... of loyalty ... and goodwill. We wish profoundly that we could be ... sure of fulfilling the hopes that you place in us ... but there are reasons that make us doubt ... whether it will . prove possible.'

The words met with an uneasy silence. The hearers were taken aback, dismayed. The High Priest's heart sank like a weighty coffin going to the bottom of the lake. 'Not now, of all times.' But Montezuma went on unchecked.

'As is already known to you, not only has the temple of the god of fire been struck by lightning and a fiery-tailed star been seen in the sky, but the smoking mirrors reveal omens of an ominous and threatening nature: those of armies marching upon our land. We too have seen and interpret these signs in the same way.'

The priests of the god of darkness and evil nodded knowingly. A quiver of uneasiness, of fear, ran through the hall. Only the Jaguar Prince, he noted, seemed unperturbed to hitch at an imaginary sword, as if to say, 'Let's get at 'em.' The Emperor's face was grave.

'Now the fateful Year One Reed approaches ... the time appointed by the god of wind and life for his return ... the year in which he has promised that he would come and take possession of our Kingdom.'

The silence that fell was as heavy as a colossal pyramid, as dark as a sealed tomb. He allowed himself a brief glance. Montezuma, who earlier had seemed cheerful and at ease, now looked sombre, apprehensive, almost despairing.

At this point the High Priest of the god of wind and life ventured to demur in deferential, tentative fashion.

'Perhaps, Your Imperial Majesty, might it not prove to be a blessing for our land to be visited by Quetzalcoatl, the Feathered Serpent?'

'Huh!' muttered the High Priest of the sun-god under his breath.

'Our writings foretell that it will be a time of great distress and even disaster for our people,' replied the Emperor seriously. 'All the signs and portents point to that.'

In the strained, soundless silence that followed, dark thoughts hovered vulture-like. The High Priest reflected, 'If he did return it would be a ticklish situation, one that would require delicate handling.'

The Emperor went on earnestly, 'If he were to do so, everything will be done to make his visit harmless or even beneficial to our land and people.'

But amid the chorus of agreement, approval and confidence in him that followed, the High Priest noticed shrewdly that Montezuma was looking around self-distrustingly, as if seeking for help and support.

Their spirits, damp and heavy as soil after a rainstorm, only lifted when the Emperor suggested some entertainments. His dwarfs and albinos trotted forward and performed their antics to the guests' delight. The hall rang with laughter. Their anxiety dispersed like smoke blown away by the wind.

5

Work and Play

He had been taken up with business all morning, money mainly. He studied the deerskin roll once more; the accounts were in a far more satisfactory state. He would have to see the Temple Treasurer shortly, that greedy, insinuating, ill-natured pest. Things were not improved by the cost of the Emperor's gift, for that banquet, which had turned out so unfortunately. Really, Montezuma's behaviour had been quite out of character, though, in view of the trend of his thinking, only to be expected. But clearly there was no cause for alarm. It was merely a matter of placating the gods by performing the sacrificial rites correctly.

Of course, if this god of wind and life were ever to return, the wisest course would be to obtain his favour by all possible means. He would advise the Emperor to do so. But, meanwhile, he had far more pressing problems on his mind.

Uneasy and fearful, the people were insatiable in their demands that more and yet more sacrifices should be offered up. Now reports were reaching him that the conquered tribes were growing restless under the levy of prisoners. Rebellions threatened. Worse, it gave great power to the war commanders. It was unbearable to have to depend on men such as the Jaguar Prince.

The Treasurer was seen, not without some tiresome misunderstandings, and dismissed, not without a sigh of relief. He returned to the overriding problem: how was he to get hold of enough victims without inflating the importance of the military, or stirring up a revolt?

His litter was borne along by four swarthy, burly porters. Riding high on it, he had a commanding view of the countryside. They had left behind them the clutter of closely packed mud and reed huts, and lofty, imposing stone buildings; and crossed the blue, sparkling Moon Lake by one of the three wide, stone causeways. Looking back the city seemed to float on the lake, as if suspended in the air. White-coloured temples and houses with gold ornamenting flashed and glinted in the brilliant sunshine. The paved road narrowed, after a time, to a dusty track between brown fields, stripped bare of their bright green and yellow maize crop. The vital spring planting with its essential festival and sacrifices was some while off; there was no need for him to remain in the capital to officiate. He could leave his worries behind and take a rest ... at last.

She would be glad to see him, in view of who he was. Did she like his gift? It was beautiful and valuable: carved jade set in gold, shaped like a flower, just right for her. He hoped to find her wearing it. (Really the Treasurer need not have made quite so much fuss about the temple funds.) But that need not be the real reason for her willingness to see him. She was lucky to have the foremost man in the realm, next to the Emperor, as her admirer. Officially members of the priesthood were celibate ... but ...

She had been paying far too much attention to that Jaguar Prince of late. He had heard that the fellow had even been giving her jewellery – the scoundrel! Really, he would stop at nothing. How unfair that he had been kept from her for so long by inescapable priestly duties. It gave his hateful rival far too much opportunity.

But now he was paying her a visit. She had invited him and it could only be for one reason: she wanted to see him. His chance had come.

17

6

The Jaguar Prince

They were sitting talking to one another. She was as beautiful and alluring as ever, but distant. The Prince's eyes fell upon her flowered gold and jade ornament. She had not been wearing that the last time he saw her ... so he had given it to her. Huh!

'I'm so glad you could spare time to come and see me before you go off to the War of the Flowers.'

'I've always time for you,' he fibbed.

But her sole response was a disbelieving yet charming smile.

The question was as prickly as any cactus.

'You've been letting him give you jewellery, haven't you?'

Did she withdraw slightly?

'He's an important man.'

'So am I – I'm related to the Emperor.'

'Really!'

That had impressed her anyway.

'One of his cousins, in fact.'

'I see,' she smiled, 'and all the victories you've won too.'

'I've had my share of them.'

He tried not to sound boastful, but he longed for her to look favourably on him. The Precious Jewel Lady was most desirable as a wife.

Earlier in the day she had taken him to see round her vast estates. (It was rather spoilt by that wretched maidservant being with them throughout. She was in the room even now. Could they never be alone? She seemed determined to make things awkward and, what was more, he felt she enjoyed doing so.) He had been shown barns bursting with maize and beans and peppers being loaded for market.

'How many field hands?' he had asked.

'Two thousand five hundred,' was the prompt answer.

Marriage would join their estates nicely and make him the richest landowner in the realm. Her brother was highly placed too. But, most of all, he found her attractive, very. What a curse that other fellow was chasing after her, a confounded nuisance, his being who he was. Had any man ever been stuck like that before, having as his rival the High Priest? Damn' sticky! As she herself had said, the man was too important to offend. Have to tread carefully. But hang it, he couldn't marry her! But was that what she wanted? All these gifts. He was just trying to buy her. What did she really want: marriage or an affair? That was the trouble with women – you didn't know what they wanted or were thinking. Either way that bastard was queering his pitch and there was no way of getting rid of him, couldn't send him off on a hopeless expedition like a common soldier. How could he make him look small in her eyes? He racked his brains.

'Darling, do you know something your fond admirer did? At that banquet I caught him looking the Emperor right in the face.'

'Really!'

Her eyes were as round as pools.

'Yes. S'pose he thinks he can get away with it, seeing who he is. Still, it's a bit much.'

'Yes, dreadful,' she almost whispered.

He noticed with satisfaction that she was shocked.

'Did you enjoy it?'

'The banquet? Yes, most of it, that is.' He paused. 'Only one fly in the ointment, His Imperial Majesty was in rather an unusual frame of mind.'

'Unusual – in what way?'

'Worried about bad omens.' She looked concerned. 'The temple of the fire god was struck by lightning some time ago.'

'So I've heard. Still, nothing awful's happened since.'

'Yes ... but then there's this fiery-tailed star.'

'Best not to let that sort of thing upset you. Harvest's all right, so why worry?'

'Yes,' she agreed softly, 'the harvest was good.'

'So long as we make enough sacrifices the gods should be happy.'

'Yes, I'm sure you're right. I always feel so sorry for the poor victims,' she added languidly.

'But necessary – must keep the sun strong.'

'Of course.'

'People have been getting in a twit for years and everything's been fine, never been better.'

'I hope you are right, Coatl.'

But by now his mind was running on other matters. 'Soon be in the field again ... they're always bellyaching for more prisoners, it's not them that has to get them – it's us. But should be no difficulty. Ha! Provinces kicking up a bit of a fuss – get the quota out of them, though, with a bit of firmness ... great life soldiering.'

She was thinking, 'Let's forget about omens. It's lovely having both of them to come and see me – and it's making dear Coatl frightfully jealous too. Hee! Hee! Did Pochtli really do something awful like that? Not that I like him very much, but he's the highest man in the land, next to the Emperor, of course, to have him paying all this attention to me, and giving me all these things ... it's far too good a chance to throw away. I couldn't just brush him off.' She came back to everyday matters.

'Jasmine, we would like our drinks of chocolate.'

They were alone.

She smiled coquettishly and asked him, 'Do you really want to go?'

'Got to, unfortunately. Don't want to leave you one bit.'

'I'll miss you.'

'You will? Will you be glad to see me back?'

'Of course I will.'

She was in an oncoming, skittish mood. Dare he try to put an arm round her?

'You're very beautiful you know – like snow upon the far-off mountains.'

She was delighted, for all her pretending not to take it seriously. Yet still she gave him no further encouragement. He was baffled.

'Your cheeks are lovelier than a hibiscus flower and your eyes are like twin stars shining in the heavens.'

'Flattery again,' she scoffed archly, but still she did not invite him to sit beside her.

He was planning his next move when Jasmine re-entered, a sly smirk on her face. 'Bother!' There was nothing else for it, now he must sit and talk about nothing in particular.

The rest of the day followed the same course. He took his leave that evening.

Her parting words were 'I am sad you have to go. Do be careful. Don't come to any harm.'

But did she mean it? What did she really feel about him?

7

A Direful Forecast

So that was it! She had been seeing that beastly Jaguar Prince once more. Odious fellow! And just how far had things gone between them? Pochtli, High Priest of the sun-god, squirmed at the thought of it. His feelings then turned to rage. That loathsome, hateful, contemptible, swaggering oaf of a soldier, so inferior to himself, had been going behind his back, had he? Creeping, worming his way into her favour, had he? And by what means too ... flattery, gifts ... promises. Unbearable! How could she entertain the thought, look at him even, when there was himself, High Priest, next in importance only to the God-Emperor, a ruler no man dare look in the face lest he be blinded? For Montezuma was the sun-on-earth.

The 'Wars of the Flowers' had begun for this year. Why then was the heroic prince not off campaigning? He would drop a word in the Emperor's ear, a sly insinuation that his highly esteemed commander was ... lacking in courage. He would be packed off to the battlefield, or made to look a fool. But he must go about it carefully. It would not do to ...

But someone sought audience with him: and no less a person than the Imperial Mathematician and Astronomer was ushered into his presence.

'Your Excellency.' The other greeted him with the merest suggestion of a bow. Then the tall, bulbous-headed visitor, in long scholar's robes, got down to business without ceremony. 'I have come to inform you of an important matter.'

'Yes. What is it?'

Wrapping himself in his dignity like a cloak, sharp nose pointing forwards, he listened impassively.

'Unusual signs have been observed in our mighty god, the sun.'

The High Priest became alert. This was important.

'What are they?'

'Certain spot-like blemishes have been observed upon his divine countenance and he is throwing out flames that reach far out into the heavens.

'Portending?'

'Heavy rains and storms of the greatest magnitude.'

'The sacrifices have been offered up in the correct manner.'

'Naturally.'

That made clear, they could get down to discussing the matter.

'When may these storms be expected?'

The other examined his deerskin parchment in a ponderously important, deliberate fashion.

'They are likely to occur sometime between the next full moon and the one thereafter.'

Right in the middle of the planting season. It could not be worse. The silence that followed was long and pregnant with thought.

'I thought it best to forewarn you.'

'The matter will be seen to.'

The High Priest spoke with cold, dispassionate reserve. The other gave him a knowing look. Did he also half smile up his sleeve? But he needed him too much to take offence.

So the responsibility was now the High Priest's. For the probable floods: the priests of the rain god could see to that problem. But sunshine was his. Would he be able to get hold of enough victims and, more, to fix exactly the right time for their sacrificing?

8

The Anger of the Gods

As forecast, the storms struck. They were sudden and devastating. It began with heavy, ceaseless, tropical rain, which made an unending pattering sound, like the beating of a thousand drums, until people were nearly crazed by it. Then the downpour grew to a deluge, as if a monster were emptying a bottomless jug of water over the world. Rivers overflowed their banks and disgorged their swollen loads into the lake. For days on end the sun was blotted out by thick, smoky layers of cloud. From time to time it struggled out weakly, fleetingly from behind the blanket of greyness, and glimmered pale, watery and wan as any moon.

Then the wind whipped up with a savage roar, like a leap of leopards, and lashed the still waters of the lake into seething white-capped waves that boiled and foamed along the shores of the island city of Tenochtitlan. Canoes were smashed to splinters, roofs blown away, huts damaged. Even hardy fishermen dared not venture out. Fed by a hundred swollen streams, the Moon Lake flooded its banks; huts and garden plots lay awash and wavelets surged even along the peaceful canals within the city.

Fear shuddered through the land. The people cried out, 'The gods are angry.' Day after day the priests of the rain-god offered sacrifices to their offended deity. There were mass stabbings, beheadings and drownings, immolations by the hundred. But still the storms vented themselves upon the land; and still the High Priest of the sun-god held his hand.

When all hoped that the storm had ended, suddenly, unexpectedly, it rose to a raging hurricane. It fell in full fury upon them. A nightmare of destruction followed. Dwellings were flattened or blown away, people injured. Some of the islands broke loose from their plant-rooted moorings and drifted off into the lake. On the mainland, peasant huts were smashed and thatched roofs caught alight in the smouldering hearth embers. Villages were swept away by raging torrents, their inhabitants drowned. The survivors fled to the hills, only returning to pick out their wretched, sodden, charred belongings from their ruined homes. In the mountains, men and beasts were struck by fire from heaven. Floods seeped across the countryside; valley bottoms lay under water. The precious, young maize plants were washed out of the soil, or battered flat to lie in sodden heaps, mildewing in pools of mud and slime. Beans and squashes rotted in the dank ooze left when the waters drained reluctantly away. Men faced homelessness, ruin.

Alarm ran through the people and their cry rose in anguish, 'The gods are angry with us.'

The moment had come. The High Priest spoke at last.

'The festival will be held at the full moon.'

9

The Children of the Sun

'Was much of the sacred victim's blood lost?' The High Priest asked sternly.

'No, not a great deal, Your Excellency. It was only through a small cut in his knee.'

The Chief Temple Priest's words tumbled out too rapidly, self-excusingly. The look of harsh disapproval on the hawk-like face of the High Priest relaxed slightly.

'How did it happen?'

'He fell from the top of the garden wall.'

'Was he trying to escape?'

'No, Your Excellency. No. No, he was only trying to reach some peaches.'

'I see.'

The faintest shadow of a leering smile ghosted across the High Priest's face.

'He wanted to eat some. The fruit is to be picked by the gardeners and brought down to them. Anything that a Child of the Sun wants he is to have.'

His voice became stern again.

'But they must not be allowed to escape.'

'Of course not, Your Excellency. We will keep a close watch on the children.' His superior glowered pointedly and he hastily corrected himself, 'On the Children of the Sun.'

The cold, critical glare smoothed away and then, speaking deliberately, with dogmatic emphasis, the High Priest laid down, 'Our god, the sun, particularly desires and rejoices in the blood of young people – their vigour enriches him and ensures his strength and power.'

'Yes, of course, Your Excellency.'

'The people must understand this.'

'Of course, Your Excellency. It will be made clear to them.'

He allowed a cold silence to show that the conversation was at an end. Bowing, the other departed. He was left to his own thoughts.

This shortage of victims ... true, three youths of noble family had come forward offering themselves. But these were only low-playing cards; a famous commander would have been preferable. The gods were demanding an exceptional sacrifice ... and he had found it for them. He smiled to himself. Not for nothing had he, after much intrigue, been appointed High Priest.

Yes, the Children of the Sun: it was a stroke of genius.

*　*　*　*　*　*

The temple gardens glowed with bright, tropical flowers in the brief, spasmodic flashes of brilliant sunshine. Its high, thick, stone walls were so hot that they pricked the fingers. Within this and the massive, stone, temple buildings, the Children of the Sun lived, cut off from the world without, never to leave until the day of their death. Within, they were allowed to roam about, playing as they chose. Indulgent priests attended them and obsequious gardeners bowed to them, complacently overlooking the damage that they did. They shook the trees until the fruit rained to the ground and the branches broke, tore up the plants and snatched the flowers in order to decorate themselves.

A small boy cried wretchedly, 'I want to go home. I want my mummy.'

'Yah! Cry-baby,' scoffed some older ones.

A sycophantly smiling attendant fed him one cacao bean after another but the child went on whining.

A screaming gang dashed past wildly. Trampling straight across the carefully tended beds, they tore the flowers to pieces in their headlong rush, pulping the beautiful blooms into the earth. They ripped the brightly coloured blossoms off the bushes and snatched and squashed the ripe fruits to pelt each other in mock battle. Scattering, they hooted mad challenges at one another. Then the mob glued together again and went surging round the enclosure like a hungry wolf pack, to swirl up against the far wall, nearly climbing it. Suddenly it turned, and howling and screeching uncontrollably, tore back towards the buildings.

A lovely teenage girl with face distraught, stood shrieking at empty air. On a whim she began plucking the red hibiscus flowers and plaiting them into her long, thick, black hair. Then unpredictably, impulsively, she ripped them to shreds and flung them to the ground, where they formed a blood red trail of wounded petals and battered blooms.

The three noble youths were throwing an orange-coloured ball to one another. Sometimes they let smaller children join in their quiet game. At others, they earnestly discussed such questions as, 'When the sun has drunk our blood, will we be able to visit the earth again in his rays?'

A youthful acolyte stepped out from one of the buildings. He was stopped by a boy who demanded to have his gold sword. Without hesitation or demur, he handed it over to him.

'For a Child of the Sun, anything,' he agreed with a smile and walked on briskly.

Nothing unusual had happened, nothing at all. The new possessor raced off with a yell of glee. Like cattle stampeding, the others tore after him, bent upon grabbing the bauble, upon having it, if only for a moment.

Overhead the sun briefly flamed fiercely, pouring hot, brilliant rays onto the steaming earth.

10

Danger from Afar

The five hundred soldiers had boarded the ships with their weapons, horses and also fourteen cannons with powder shot. Sweating and swearing, the sailors hauled the huge square sails up the masts. The wind nearly dragged the ropes out of their hands; they were caught, tamed and made fast. The ships surged forward like birds in undulating flight, shuddering slightly under the shock of the waves. The busy island of Cuba sank out of sight behind them.

Heedless of their Spanish homeland lying thousands of miles astern, the hardy conquerors were exulting. They had already subdued the islands of the West Indies for God, and the King of Spain and enriched themselves. Now, their leader, the bravest of men, was promising them fresh conquests, greater riches. For ahead, on the mainland, the Aztec Empire possessed gold beyond their most heated dreams. More, so it was said, its people believed that a 'white god' would return to them to claim his kingdom, and in this very year. Conquest could be easy. The veterans licked their lips in anticipation.

On the spray-spattered deck of the leading ship, resolute, indominatable, stood Cortés.

11

Sacrificed to the Sun-God

The children were awakened one morning early by the sound of trumpets blowing atop the pyramid. Clad in white robes, they were led into the great hall by deferentially bowing, smiling attendants. There they were given a meal of chocolate dainties and a drink, strange to the taste. Except for one small boy, who was sick, their behaviour then began to change in curious fashion. The petty, furtive whispering and nervous quarrelsome restlessness gave way to floating gestures and carefree giggling. Then a feverish jollity seized them. They played hectically, shouting with raucous, inane laughter.

When the gloating, fawning attendants came to conduct them from the place, they broke loose. Pressing ahead of them eagerly with cheeks aglow and eyes on fire, they rushed in a throng up the steep slope that led to the pyramid steps.

The huge square was crammed with worshippers, already excited by the sight of blood. Now it was noon, the sun had wrestled its way out from behind smutty clouds and was throwing bright, sharp rays onto the blood-soaked scene. The pinnacle of the shrine cast a short, black, sinister shadow across the altar.

Suddenly the onlookers' obscenely fascinated attention was distracted by the unexpected sound of singing and laughter and the Children of the Sun burst upon their astonished gaze. Like moths drawn to a flame, they came. Nothing could have checked or diverted them. Pushing each other to get there first, they rushed up the pyramid steps and, scrambling out onto its lower platform, took possession of it. Startled, the people stared up at them. The masked dancers ceased their endless twirling. The musicians fell silent.

As they stood gaping, the sacred victims, led by the leering priest, linked hands to form a circle, symbol of the sun. The circle began wheeling slowly. Round and round it turned. Faster and faster it spun. Nearly delirious with unnatural joy, the children danced round, whirling faster and faster, and as they danced they sang,' The sun-god, the sun-god!'

There was a second of awed silence, then the drummers picked up the rhythm. 'The sun-god! The sun-god!' The other music makers joined in; the masked dancers leapt and twisted once again. The crowd stirred, drawn into it. The tide of excitement rose.

A victim was pulled out. Instantly, the broken circle reformed. The rest danced on heedlessly carefree, rapturously indifferent to their fate.

With face alight, the one chosen glided serenely up the flight of steps. She stretched herself willingly along the altar. The end was swift and bloody. Her screams were drowned by the drums.

In turn, each of the three noble youths were escorted deferentially up the steps by the chanting priests. They died with dignity, seemingly indifferent to pain.

The watchers' gaze was riveted by the loathsome spectacle. As youthful chests were ripped open and pulsating hearts held aloft spurting blood, a thrill of depraved delight, like an electric charge, ran through them. Faces gloated with obscene joy; excitement swelled to frenzy. Drunk with bloodlust, they were swept up into the chanting: 'The sun-god! The sun-god!'

The blazing sun scorched down, soaking up the gore. Clots dripped from the quartz knife, the altar ran blood. The pyramid steps lay steaming, slippery with it. Pools of blood collected flies and the rank smell of blood cloyed the nostrils. Still the Children of the Sun circled tirelessly, heedlessly, still

31

they laughed and sang. Hysteria swept the worshippers. 'The sun-god! The sun-god!' they raved.

The fever spread. The High Priest, aloof on the pyramid top, was caught up in it. He worked on with deadly skill, but bloodlust was gripping him. With eyes staring demoniacally, he tore out bleeding, beating hearts for offering to the idols that leered down unseeing. He was flintily indifferent to the look of anguish in the young victims' eyes when the dread moment of death came. He was as deaf to their shrill screams of agony as he would be to the cries of gulls at the distant coast. The gods needed food; the sun must have human blood to drink. The circle dwindled, melted. One by one the children were stretched out on the altar and butchered.

The last was a beautiful teenage girl. She wore a hibiscus flower in her long black hair. It was blood red. She was terrified. Her screams split the heads of the hearers.

That left the adults. They waited in terror, but too crushed in spirit to try to escape. One after another they were driven up the steps, dragged onto the alter, tied down and slaughtered.

Darkness fell. Thousands of flickering flares cast a glimmer of light that sent weird rippling shadows coiling across the ghastly scene. In the deathly glow, blood spurted, oozed, dripped, trickled, spattered and finally congealed. The desultory, slow heaviness of the sultry late afternoon fled. The zest of the crowd sharpened once more. As victim after victim was slaughtered, the tempo of the orgy quickened, rising to an ecstatic frenzy. Beside themselves, the watchers were pricking themselves with needles and cutting themselves with knives. One man slit his jugular vein. The blood gushed forth, soaking his tunic front, and poured out like a flood onto the paving stones.

Prisoner after prisoner was dispatched. Blood dripped from the altar; it ran down the pyramid in streams. Bloodlust held the worshippers in its unholy grip. They were enslaved by devilish forces that made them surge to and fro, screaming as if possessed, and all the while they raved hysterically, 'The sun-god! The sun-god! The sun-god!'

The mass madness continued without ceasing until the last victim had been murdered.

*   *   *   *   *   *

Next day the temple garden lay empty, silent as a tomb. Only the slow, placid gardeners toiled at the task of tidying it.

Over it a deathly, void heaviness hung vulture-like, brooded thickly in the air.

12

Rivalry

He had every cause for feeling triumphant. The people were calmed and satisfied. More, he had 'wiped the eye' of his hated rivals, those priests of the god of darkness and evil. For if the blood of a famous military leader was beneficial to the gods, how much more must be that of dozens of young and vigorous people?

The storms had ceased, of course. For a short while after the ceremony the sky had been a sullen, dirty grey, or dense with dark clouds threatening more rain. But little fell.

'When our god, the sun, has digested the feast we have given him, he will shine,' he assured them.

A few days later, the clouds broke up and floated away. The sun glided out triumphantly, to shine in splendour from a sky that was a bowl of brazen blue. Hot, brilliant rays probed finger-like into the soaking, steaming earth.

'Naturally,' he said smugly. 'What else did you expect?'

*   *   *   *   *   *

He could leave the daily sacrifice of a single victim, to ensure that the sun would rise each morning, to his subordinate. At last he was free from fasting and ceremonies. Should he pay her another visit? She had dropped more than a hint that she would like to see him again. Why delay, then, and let that scoundrel of a Prince get in first?

*   *   *   *   *   *

The Moon Lake shimmered a deep blue, sparkling in the brilliant sunshine; its wavelets flashed a thousand tiny, white, scintillating diamonds. The peasants in the sodden fields pointed him out to their children, bowing low to him as he was borne past. He did not deign to acknowledge or even notice them.

His mind was full of lecherous thoughts, lascivious imaginings. He would be seeing her soon ... her exquisite face, shapely, enticing body ... embracing it perhaps ... to have her. Would she be in willing mood, or cool and distant? It was all very teasing. Was she only flirting with him, leading him on like this? Doubtless she would like the gold bracelet with feather design. Perhaps it would soften her towards him. But that beastly Prince was worming his way into her affections ... the swine. But he would put him down. Falling Eagle Prince was deeply jealous of him. He had played on that, dropped words in his ear. Now he could sit back and watch what would happen.

Meanwhile, he would take a pleasant holiday. As far as everyone knew, he was coming to review the finances of the local temple, but in reality ...

*   *   *   *   *   *

He was torn by conflict between delight at seeing her again and exasperation and hurt at the way she had treated him. At one minute she had been so warm, inviting and responsive, the next, cool and uninterested. He was rebuffed, at a loss.

She had accepted the gold bracelet gladly and put it on straightaway, but that was all. Did she not realise his importance? Something, apart from the other man, stood in the way. He sensed that she was afraid of him. People usually were. He did not care. He enjoyed it; it pandered to his love of power. But in her case, it might spoil everything. She might shy off him altogether. He must try to persuade her, reassure her, that

35

beneath the High Priest's robes he was like any other man, that he had the same desires, but was able to offer higher rewards.

Then another disquieting thought struck him: was she really in love with that Prince? Horror upon horror, if she were . . .

As the litter bore him back towards the capital, he was tortured by jealousy. He dreamed of revenge.

13

In More Than One Mind

The Precious Jewel Lady lay on her couch daydreaming. It was all very interesting, flattering too, to have someone like him begging for her favours. More than one of her friends had remarked on it with a touch of envy. How the news had got about! Nice present this bracelet. Of course, he was only after one thing, anyone could see. She was not at all sure about him. Dear Coatl, pity he was away fighting. How madly jealous he would be if he knew. It was all too delightful ...

As High Priest, Pochtli could make the sun shine. Such power, it was quite frightening. But now she was seeing him 'in undress', so to speak, and he was all too weak and human, like other men.

What did other women see in him? Power. He was rich, of course, and clever too. She wondered who his present concubine was. Gossip said ... But perhaps there was none at present and that was why he was paying her so much attention. She turned the possibility over in her mind. One does not embark upon an affair without first making quite sure.

She dozed off to sleep and from the mind's dark, fetid depths, hidden memories floated upwards as dreams, like bubbles bursting on the surface of the lake. Childhood ... the gigantic blood-stained pyramid overawing them ... high above their heads, the High Priest standing dominant, with the power to give life, to destroy it ... The helpless victim stretched out before him, on the altar. She watched riveted, fascinated. With the long knife he cut through the membrane ... a scream of agony ... blood trickling, streaming through the rent ... pouring from it, pumping, gushing from the beating heart he held high. But with a stab of horror she suddenly saw the High Priest to be Pochtli ... and herself the victim! The knife was raised. The yell of the crowd threw back her own shrill shriek of terror. But no cry came, it was but a croaking whisper. She gave a sharp jerk ... and slowly swam back to wakefulness ... only a dream. How silly! Why should she feel afraid just because ...? Really, there was no need for this uneasy feeling that he gave her. Besides, it would not do to offend anyone so important. What was wrong with a little dalliance so long as one's own feelings were not involved?

But at the same time she wished deeply that Coatl were there with her.

14

The Return of the God

'I will return in Year 1 Reed and re-establish my rule. It will be a time of great trouble for my people.' The Feathered Serpent god

*   *   *   *   *   *

So the direful portents were right, the smoking mirrors had told no lies.

The white god had come back to them, sailing up from the paradise of the sun in the eastern ocean, whither he had taken himself long, long ago. More, he had kept his every promise: to arrive on his name day, in Year 1 Reed, wearing black and with a plumed headdress.

In the capital they were as disturbed and agitated at the news as an overturned hive of bees. At first there had been hopes that he would be satisfied with the treasure that the Emperor had given him and go away once more. But instead, he had waited for an invitation that was never made and burnt the strange, huge canoes in which he had come. So he meant to stay. Then the god informed them that he meant to pay a visit to their capital.

Consternation filled the Emperor, his priests and councillors alike. What could they do to placate a god who refused human sacrifices? His coming might mean war in the heavens, disaster upon earth.

15

Young Love

Petl sat high on the litter beside her betrothed, Tizoc. They were to have been married, by their parents' arrangement, in a few weeks' time. Then, suddenly, disaster had struck. The fateful lot had fallen on them. They were among those to be sacrificed at the midsummer festival. Weeping wretchedly, the young pair had said farewell to their heartbroken parents and now, along with the others, were being taken away, escorted by soldiers, to the far-off capital, from which they would never return.

The chosen victims rode in state, adorned with jewellery, bedecked with flowers, that the people had showered upon them. At length the hated Aztec city came in sight. Swimming in the lake mist, it rose out of the water, a place of dread. It crouched sinister, threatening, like a sharp-clawed lion, intent to maul, devour.

The bearers carried the young captives across the milelong stone causeway that led straight into the broad street, a wide open mouth, waiting to swallow. Petl darted frightened glances ahead. She was dismayed, alarmed.

'Horrible place. I don't like it,' she said with a shudder. 'It scares me.'

Tizoc tried to hide his fears.

'It's foreign – theirs,' was all he said.

There was a sudden cry and a loud splash. A youth had broken loose and flung himself into the lake. He was drowned. The soldiers guarded the rest more watchfully.

Petl and Tizoc were carried into the city. It seethed with gawping, gloating people. Her eyes grew round and large.

'Look at them all.'

'Too many and all Aztecs,' said Tizoc with hatred, then added glumly, 'No chance of our fighting our way out.'

They crossed the canals that served as streets and came to the market square. The blood-drenched pyramid dominated it.

'Oh! No! Look!' cried Petl and covered her face with her hands and even Tizoc turned away in fear.

The huge stone temple stood at the corner. The heavy gates of gold were flung wide open. The couple were carried under its wide, echoing archway into the courtyard within its thick, high walls, as if sucked into a monster's stomach. The gates were fastened behind them. Quietness fell. The restless, noisy bustle of the outside world vanished from sight, from hearing.

They were not kept waiting long. Adulating priests and fawning attendants welcomed them with bows and smirks, giving them good food and showing them to clean beds, and, to their surprise and delight, the next day, every day, was the same. They were decked out in jewels and fine new clothes, delicious meals were served and dainties pressed upon them. Their every whim was pandered to, every wish fulfilled.

Some of their uneasy fear fell away. Once more, the immense, cold, still building clattered with the noise of youthful feet and the garden rang to childish screams and laughter.

*　　*　　*　　*　　*　　*

The boy crouched behind the dense bushes.

'Watch out, you awful lot ... me and me chums are waitin' fer yer ... real ambush, like wot father and uncle go on. Yer lot only cum here yesterday ... an' no one wants yer. They're creeping' this way ... wait a mo... Now! C'mon warriors! Up and bash 'em.'

41

Lumps of hard earth flew through the air, followed by a hail of stones.

'Yah! Look at 'em! Runn'n fer it ... Yah! Softies ... after 'em ... shy some more at 'em. Gotem! Hooray!'

*   *   *   *   *   *

'How did it happen?'

The High Priest looked stern.

'We don't know, Your Excellency. It seems a quarrel broke out among the Children of the Sun and ...'

'Which of them started it?'

'We think, Your Excellency, the boys of the Silver Fox tribe and the Mountain Leopard tribe. They are always at war with one another.'

'I know that.'

'And then, Your Excellency, it turned into a fight and one or two, not many, got hurt.'

'Has much blood been wasted?'

'Oh no, Your Excellency, not much. That is ... Only a little, Your Excellency. The bleeding was quickly stopped.'

'They must be punished,' rapped the High Priest curtly. 'And it must not happen again.'

The pampered Children of the Sun discovered, to their surprise, that they too could be smacked and sent to bed like ordinary children.

*   *   *   *   *   *

They were in the garden together. The sun blazed hotly upon a riot of crimson and yellow blossom, scarlet and white flowers.

Tizoc smiled delightedly and put his arm round Petl's waist. Her dark eyes flashed coyly up at him.

'Let's be together.'

'Should we?' she asked.

42

'You would have been my bride.'

'Yes.' She looked sad. 'Where shall we go?'

'No one will see us in there.'

He pushed his way into the thick bushes, holding her by the hand. She giggled shyly.

The heavy sweet-scented blooms glowed like thousands of rubies and pearls amid the dark leaves. In their midst was a cool gloom.

They could find no words in which to express their feelings. He put his arms round her. They kissed with growing feeling, then lay close together on the moist, dark earth.

'I wonder what Mother would say,' Petl said and then giggled.

'She's not here to tell us off.'

They kissed passionately, then with abandoned joy.

'Let's be together tonight,' he whispered.

'Where?'

'Anywhere, as long as we're alone.'

She thought hard, then her dark eyes lit up.

'I'll ask if I can have the room at the end of the building, you know the one. It belongs to the priest who's always giving us things.'

'Good.' He gave her a tight squeeze and whispered softly, 'I'll be coming to see you.'

*   *   *   *   *   *

Within the dim gloom of the temple itself, the idols stood menacingly. There were idols of seeds glued together with human blood, idols of wood and stone, gold-masked, blood-smeared. From on high, the fearful gods of war leered down evilly.

Petl, inquisitive, had strayed in there once – and fled in fear. She shuddered at the thought of the place.

Dusk and close darkness. It was him tapping softly on the door. She opened it.

43

He was standing there, tall and strong, her darling Tizoc. He stepped into the room. They both laughed gleefully, mischievously, and he took her in his arms.

'Darling,' she breathed, 'you've come.'

'As I promised,' he said.

'Now we can be together. No one will know.'

'They won't find out,' he chortled.

Lying on the couch, kissing passionately, they entered their short-lived paradise.

16

Together to the Last

Cool dawn was long past. The sun beat down with vicious strength. Its brilliant rays outlined the pyramid starkly, so that its hard flint-like edges sawed the clear, pale blue sky.

The Children of the Sun surged up the steps and out onto the platform. From below, the worshippers stared up at them, gloating obscenely. Laughing carefreely, the young people joined hands. The circle began to wheel round. They were dancing and singing. Faster and faster the wheel spun and louder and louder they laughed and sang in excited rapture. Hair flying and white robes swirling, they whirled in their circle – the sacred circle of the sun.

The gruesome ritual began. Astounded at first, the people gazed in silence. Then, mesmerised by the drumbeat, inflamed by the sight of blood, they became exalted, intoxicated and began chanting, 'The sun-god! The sun-god!'

Petl's fears had melted like a mist lifting. She floated softly up the steps in a tranquil trance. Breaking out of the ring, Tizoc glided up too. He could not bear to be parted from her. They stood beside each other, hand in hand, at the blood-soaked altar. She stretched herself out on it without a tremor. He joined her. They lay beside each other.

The High Priest raised the knife. The drumbeats crescendoed to a deafening tattoo. There were gasps and screams that no one heard, and then blood spurting from the two beating hearts, mingling together in his hands, then in the sacred casket, onto the mound of slithery flesh before the idols.

The Children of the Sun were butchered to the last one. The dancers gyrated like whipped tops; the drummers beat out their frenzied stacatto rhythm. The peoples' excitement rose. Men were slashing themselves, spilling their lifeblood. The pile of corpses grew to mountains. Vültures wheeled overhead, hawking harsh cries. Steeped, caked in human blood, the towering white pyramid loured over them menacingly, hideously.

The slaughter of the prisoners went on mercilessly the rest of the day. As the last victims were sacrificed, the onlookers' bloodlust was whipped up to a climax of frenzy. 'The sun-god! The sun-god!' they howled.

Dusk came down like a curtain of death. Slowly, the madness ebbed, died away. The onlookers drifted away, drained, exhausted. A sick silence fell. Darkness gripped the land.

The bodies of the Children of the Sun, loaded with bracelets of silver and necklaces of gold, jewels of jade and ornaments of turquoise and lapis lazuli, lay twisted, intertwined with one another in the seeping, trickling heap.

Petl and Tizoc were close. Their hands touched, clasped each other's – in death as in life.

17

Intrigue and Rivalry

He sat looking at her longingly. She was very beautiful, very desirable. He wanted to sit next to her, to take her in his arms. But that confounded maid of hers was in the room. Didn't the wretched girl have any work to do?

Judging by her cat-like smile, the Precious Jewel Lady seemed to be enjoying the situation, he thought sulkily.

'I'm so glad you're back safely, Coatl.'

His mood changed.

'Yes, it's been a great campaign. We've not crushed those beastly Tlaxcalans yet, but there's always next year. Sent hundreds of prisoners up to the capital, bagged my share, so hope his high-priestship is satisfied.'

His tone was sardonic. She was shocked.

'Is it true, the rumours I've heard?' she asked.

'Which ones? There're always so many.'

She flashed a smile, then grew serious.

'About the god. Is he really coming to our land?'

'Seems like it. He's taking a long way round to get here, though.'

He turned it over in his mind. 'Why cross the mountains and desert instead of coming straight, unless he wants to gain allies. Some rebellious tribes, drat them, were all too ready to join him ... but then would a god need human help?'

'There don't seem to be many of them,' he said.

'No.' She looked relieved. 'But a god ...'

'If he is one.'

'Don't you think he must be?'

'Not sure about it. The Emperor thinks so ... believes him to be the god of wind and life.'

Her eyes opened wide.

'Really! Does he?'

'Seems sure of it. If not, and he's an enemy, now would be the time to attack him. Still, we outnumber them and we've never been beaten yet.'

'No, I'm sure he must be a god.'

'Hmm, maybe you're right. The high-ups must know best.'

'Of course.'

Inwardly, he thought, 'Anyway, if the Emperor's made up his mind, that settles the matter.'

She sent Jasmine off to cook their meal. Now was his chance. He was hopeful. But before he could say, 'How lovely you are,' she asked him, 'How are things for you?'

'Wonderful ... now I'm with you.'

She was triumphant, but her next question annoyed him.

'You're jealous of Pochtli, aren't you?' she teased archly.

'More than that. I'm downright angry with him.'

'Really!'

She froze like a startled rabbit.

'I've cause. He's been poisoning people's minds against me.'

'No! Whose?'

'Chiefly Falling Eagle's and it won't take long to reach the ears of the Emperor, either; all a pack of lies too.'

Her eyes were as round as those of a frightened deer.

'But it might do you harm.'

'It will. Falling Eagle's a powerful man and he's jealous of me.'

He puffed himself out. 'Knows I'm a better commander, taken more prisoners. He'd welcome a chance to do me down.'

'That mustn't happen.'

'I'd rather it didn't.'

Her brows furrowed, then cleared, and she said, 'I know, I'll get my brother, Green Jade Lord, to put in a good word for you.'

'Would it carry any weight?'

'It should. He's an Eagle Knight.'

'I see. Then it should.'

'And in favour.'

'So much the better.'

'It's very kind of you, my Precious Jewel Lady.'

She smiled bewitchingly and said, 'I'm so glad to help you, Coatl, dear. Do call me "Jewel".'

She must care about me then, he thought, his heart rising. He smiled back and, going over to her, took her tiny, dainty hands in his huge, clumsy, broad ones. He kissed her and was about to embrace her when the door opened and Jasmine re-entered, hiding a smile.

'Bother!'

But the meal was good.

* * * * * *

The High Priest's thoughts as he was carried along, were mixed.

On both sides as far as the eye could see, seas of soft greenish-white tassels flowed from the tips of swelling green sheaths, like tiny waterfalls. The maize was fast ripening to yellow plumpness in the scorching sunshine. He looked round with satisfaction. Not for nothing had their forbears swooped down from the arid deserts of the north, and seeing the promised omen of an eagle standing on a cactus devouring a snake, had decided to settle. It proved a wise choice. The land was fertile beyond their dreams; mines of gold and silver enriched it further. Conquests brought hordes of slaves to work for them, a stream of victims for sacrificing. Their numbers had swelled to millions; the upper class glutted in prosperity and privilege; the priesthood was wealthy, learned, all-powerful. Truly, the Sun-god had favoured them. Which was only to be expected: he always carried out the necessary sacrifices in exemplary fashion.

But now he was free and on his way to see her. What joy! This time she would be more loving towards him and then ...

As for his rival, those words dropped in the ear of Falling Eagle Prince would bear fruit. The man was bitterly envious and easily flattered ... but unfortunately loath to act. The Jaguar Prince, he pointed out, was the best commander they had and high in His Imperial Majesty's favour. But given time, he would destroy the fellow yet and then ...

They passed into the courtyard. He started. No! He was ... stepping out of her house. He had been seeing her, the sly loathsome creature ... worming his way into her favour ... He scrambled off his litter. The other faced him. The two men stood glaring viciously at one another. Neither spoke.

The Prince did not move aside to let him pass. His hand dropped to his dagger. 'He won't dare,' he thought, but the commander's face held neither respect nor fear of him, only anger and hatred. He glowered back.

The Prince suddenly turned away, leapt onto his litter and was borne out under the archway. Dust swirled up as he passed along the track.

The look of rage on Pochtli's face turned to a sneer.

18

The Arrival of the God

The capital seethed with the news. With his tiny force the god had defeated an immense army of Tlaxcalans. The people were torn between joy that their age-old enemy had been beaten and fear of what would happen. The victor then acted in an extraordinary fashion. He won the defeated tribe over to his side, but refused the offer of their army to fight against their hated enemy, the Aztecs.

The council meetings that followed were lengthy, anxious and divided. The military leaders wanted to attack immediately, before he reached the city. But the councillors and priests, led by the High Priest himself, advised receiving the god peacefully.

The Emperor had made up his mind.

'He must be the god of wind and life, the Feathered Serpent himself. To fight against him would prove a disaster.'

It was finally agreed that he should be allowed to enter the city. The Emperor himself and his sons would go out to welcome him.

*   *   *   *   *   *

The strange, white-faced, bearded god entered the capital, leading his laughably small army. Some were riding curious beasts like sweating, snorting stags. Others dragged a huge object that made a great flash and bang and, volcano fashion, spewed out lumps of rock-like round pieces of lava. Only a handful of Tlaxcalan guides and porters came too.

51

The Emperor, clad in his finest robes and with his sons, went out to greet them.

He descended from his rich, canopied litter to do so and welcomed the god with the words, 'Our lord, you are weary. The journey has tired you but you have arrived on the earth. You have come here to sit on your throne, to sit under its canopy.'

The speech was translated by a woman from one of the conquered tribes who accompanied the strangers. The people stood staring, silent, amazed. The guests were then shown to one of the imperial palaces, where they took up their residence.

So the god of wind and life had come back to his kingdom.

19

The Autumn Festival

The city hummed like a disturbed beehive. Men asked fearfully, 'What will happen next?'

But life must go on.

The approach of the Autumn Festival took up all the High Priest's time. There were enough prisoners, but that did not prevent the Chief Temple Priest coming up with a tiresome problem.

'Your Excellency, one of the Children of the Sun has brought a puppy with him.'

'So! A Child of the Sun may have anything he wants.' ('Why did the fellow have to trouble him with trivialities?')

'Yes, indeed, Your Excellency, yes, indeed, but he insists that it is sacrificed with him.' There was a pause while he digested this, then he laid down, 'They may be sacrificed together then. The dog's blood will feed our god, the sun, along with that of its master.'

'Very good, Your Excellency.'

He changed the subject quickly. There was no point in provoking questions about the subject.

Business done, his mind turned to his unwelcome encounter with the Jaguar Prince. So, not only had the fellow been there seeing her, but he had refused to get out of his, the High Priest's, way. And the look of hate he had given him too … nearly threatened him with violence. The insolence of it! Who was this jumped-up soldier to thwart him? Loathing and scorn raged through him.

Well, the Prince had been heard rashly saying that it would be wiser to attack the strangers now that they were inside the city. This despite the Emperor's known views on the subject. As if one could attack a god with impunity! The man was mad and best out of the way. Perhaps if Falling Eagle came to hear of it, he would hesitate no longer. Yes, he would repeat his words and in that way destroy the Prince.

* * * * * *

It was all-important; the harvest must be good.

The prisoners were brought forward; the lips of the idols were smeared with blood. The ritual began at dawn. Again, the Children of the Sun danced their circle, singing with heedless gaiety, until all had been slaughtered. As before, the worshippers, obscenely excited by the sight of blood, fell to chanting in rhythm with them.

The sun swung slowly downwards from the zenith, its rays of fire scorching the baked earth and sweating people. The heap of oozing bodies grew into a tangled mountain and among them the bejewelled Children of the Sun were strewn, still bleeding. The small boy lay face down, squashed in the bloody mêlée, his arm limp, his dead puppy tossed side.

Once again, as darkness fell, the worshippers' bloodlust became frenzied, until they were howling hysterically, 'The sun-god! The sun-god!'

The strange god and his soldiers stood watching from afar. But they were not swept up in the frenzy. Instead, amazement, then disgust and contempt filled their pale, hairy faces. Slowly their feelings heated to indignation. Finally anger and rage seized them. Going to their leader, they begged him, 'Let us kill these murderous priests. They worship devils.' But Cortés refused sternly.

'No. That would provoke the people to turn and attack us. In time they will come to believe in the One True God and our Saviour Jesus Christ, throw down their idols and forsake their evil ways.'

He had led them through direst danger and hardship, brought them victory despite unimaginable odds and promised them riches beyond belief. So, trusting their commander, his soldiers obeyed him.

20

Montezuma and the God

Disturbing rumours were reaching the High Priest's ears. Montezuma was not merely paying the god every honour, he was deferring to his every wish. He had already showered him and his greedy followers with gifts of gold and slaves, jewels of jade, a turquoise serpent brooch, a necklace of gold shrimps. But the god did not seem satisfied. Even though he had seen for himself that the Emperor ruled well and wisely, he showed no willingness to depart.

At the last audience with him, the High Priest saw that Montezuma was unsure of himself and troubled in mind. The priest had cause for deeper concern and uneasiness a few days later. To the triumphant joy of the priests of the Feathered Serpent, the god was telling the Emperor that sacrificing humans was wicked. Worse, he was trying to persuade him to give up the gods of his people and worship his one and only god. That must mean himself. But there could be no more human sacrifices and that meant the sun would die. It meant the end of the world.

Montezuma had firmly refused, with the words, 'Let us hear no more about it.'

But for how long would he do so?

Worse, the princess Malinche or 'Tongue,' who translated for the god, was taking his side more and more. The strangers esteemed her highly, despite her being their prisoner, even giving her a name: Doña Marina. And she was loyal to him. He was aware that during his all-too-frequent audiences with

Montezuma, she would add her own advice and entreaties to his. She was a dangerous enemy, like a snake coiled on the altar. Indeed, the servants who waited on them in their palace whispered that she was more to him than just an interpreter.

Something else: why did the god's followers not treat him as a god? They never bowed to him, they offered him no sacrifices, and spoke to him as if he were a mere man. They even looked him straight in the face. A god who refused to be treated as a god. Curious.

Perhaps then, he was no god at all – if that were so, it would end his power, break his hold over the Emperor.

But Montezuma would never believe it.

21

Love and Intrigue

See her he must. It was torture for the High Priest to be without her.

She welcomed him charmingly enough and accepted the gold necklace he gave her, with suitable thanks; but to his dismay she seemed more pleased with the gift than with his being there.

His hopes were high. They sat talking; his desires rose to a pitch. But her warm, enticing skittishness soon faded and she became cool and bored and their conversation lapsed into brief exchanges. Finally, he was doing all the talking, while she listened with pointed indifference.

He tried sitting nearer to her and taking her hands in his. It was worse than useless. She merely shied away and a dark look came over her face.

She watched him warily from under lowered lids. She had found out something about him. It was not that she objected to such things; she knew that men were like that. But he had been doing so while telling her that he loved only her. He was false. She felt hurt, humiliated and that she could no longer trust him. And really now he was behaving as if she belonged to him, as if she had no right to say 'no'. He had the temerity to try putting his hands on her, to fondle her, and with Jasmine in the room too, luckily. It offended her. She felt a little frightened.

She let a chilly silence fall. At last he realised that she did not want him there any longer and took his leave. She heaved a sigh of relief, rather to her own surprise. Having an admirer who was so important was wonderful, but secretly she hoped that he would not come again.

He brooded ill-temperedly about their friendship. Women were impossible! Small wonder he usually preferred boys. But now Feathered Boy, that vain, foppish youth, had started an affair with Falling Eagle of all people. It would be him. Their relations were strained anyway and this could upset all his plans.

Why had she suddenly changed towards him? Was the gift not good enough? No, it must be the Prince. Otherwise, she would love him. He must get rid of the fellow. His scheme might work yet ... despite Feathered Boy!

22

Crisis

As Pochtli feared, Falling Eagle had no wish to speak to him again, or even to see him. While he wrestled wrathfully with the problem, he learnt with surprise that Wise Lord Prince sought audience with him. It must be something important. A capable commander, a councillor of middle years and sound judgement, he was among the highest in the land.

After preliminary courtesies, the Prince of dark, sanguine features and deformed left arm came to the point without ado.

'Something serious has arisen, Your Excellency.'

'Yes, my Lord Prince.'

'It concerns the so-called god.'

'Yes.'

Most things did these days.

'He is trying to persuade His Imperial Majesty to take up residence with him in his palace.'

'That would not be at all desirable.'

'Most ill-advised. It is understood that he would continue to rule as Emperor, but under the circumstances ...'

'He would be too much under the god's influence.'

'Far too much.'

The same thought came to both of them. He would be ruling through him!

'Just so.'

But what did the Prince want him to do about it?

'We can't let it happen,' Wise Lord went on.

'Has he agreed to go?'

'Not so far. But he has offered to let his son and daughter reside with him.'

'Has he?'

That was bad news indeed.

'Yes, he must be advised most strongly not to go himself.'

'You are right.'

'I have done so already. Now there is only one person left who can persuade him.'

'You?'

'Yourself, Your Excellency. You are the High Priest. He will listen to you.'

There was a long pause while he thought hard.

Finally, he said, 'I will agree with all you say, my Lord Prince. I will consider the best way to approach His Imperial Majesty on the matter.'

* * * * * *

Sleepless nights followed. This was outrageous; it must not be allowed. The Emperor was in great danger, but how was he, Pochtli, going to persuade him to resist the god? Could he tell him that the sun god forbade his going? But this was the god of wind and life. But to give in to this insulting demand would prove a disaster. Whichever way he looked, there seemed to be only a brick wall.

As he tossed and turned restlessly, his own troubles rose in a miasma, like a swarm of flies, to distract him. The Precious Jewel Lady no longer loved or wanted him. That contemptible, hateful Prince had come between them. He could not get rid of him ... thanks to the fickleness of Feathered Boy. Falling Eagle was no help now. He was deserted.

His feelings tormented him – fretfulness, annoyance, chagrin, hurt, anger, jealousy, hatred and anxiety giving way to fear. He was nearly desperate.

Wise Lord looked to him to save them all. But how could he

tell him that it was almost impossible? He knew Montezuma's mind better than anyone else. How could he persuade him to stand firm against the god? Would he believe if told that the sun-god ordered him to refuse?

Tomorrow was the vital audience with the Emperor.

* * * * * *

The High Priest drank the potion. Was there an evil gleam in the medicine priest's eyes as he gave it to him? Impossible! Just because he had seduced the fellow's sister, a long while ago, was no reason to fear what he might do now.

Ah! What relief! A sense of comfort ... tension, anxiety were easing. Fraught feelings softly fading away. Difficulties were now pointless, meaningless. A dreamy haze lapped him about. Now he was floating away, being carried far from it all: problems, disappointments, worries, agony had vanished into nothingness. He was being wafted up by warm breezes, borne up and up to the white, soft, billowy, feathery clouds far above the earth, rocking gently to and fro as if in a canoe on the still lake. Now he was far out in the heavens, drifting further and further from the earth, being drawn towards the sun. Now he was circling, round it, whirling faster and faster ... helplessly spinning, swirling, eddying round the blazing iridescent, incandescent orb.

He awoke. It was late. He was borne to the palace in haste, there to learn that the Emperor had already left. The stranger had told him that it was the 'will of the gods' that he should go.

So Montezuma was now living with the Feathered Serpent.

23

The Crumbling Begins

It was happening, just as the High Priest had feared. The Emperor was giving in to the god's demands. He pressed precious gifts upon him and his grasping followers; finally he gave them his entire treasury. But still they were not satisfied; nor did they go away. Their enemies were punished. The Jaguar Prince was dismissed. But while he gloated over his rival's downfall, he feared for the kingdom.

There was only one consolation: Montezuma still refused resolutely to forsake the gods of his people, or end the essential human sacrifices. But he allowed the strangers to put up their own idol, a goddess they called the Virgin Mary, holding her baby, and a cross in the city, next to the temple. The common people were gawping at their ceremonies and saying that the cross made the same pattern as the arrows shot by the god of wind and life before he left their land long ago. But far worse followed.

A certain war leader had attacked a band of the strangers, who were living at the coast. Defeated, he was brought to the capital for punishment. The god ordered that he should be burnt alive. But more horrible still, he compelled His Imperial Majesty, the Emperor himself, to watch and, lest he escape, he chained his feet. Hideous and shameful! Montezuma was disgraced, humiliated, made a captive, and in the sight of his own subjects!

The people stared in horror, bewildered, terrified. Now they felt leaderless and lost. Pochtli himself knew that Montezuma was no longer the Courageous Lord who had so often led them to victory, but a broken man. It would be useless to urge him to return to his own palace now, even though the god had said he might.

Montezuma was now only the shadow of an Emperor. It was the god who ruled.

24

Love and Duty

'It's too bad of His Imperial Majesty to treat you like this and after all you've done for him, Coatl dear.'

Her voice was tender. She gazed at the tough, muscular commander.

'It's that so-called god.'

They both paused, unable to find words to express their uneasiness and fear.

'Still, it's worth it, if I can see you more often.'

'Flatterer,' she chided archly.

'There's something else: I've a feeling Falling Eagle and your precious Pochtli aren't on the best of terms these days.'

'No?'

She thought shrewdly, there was only one possible reason for that: Feathered Boy.

'Can't make it out. They were as thick as thieves a while back. Still, it won't do me any harm.'

'No. I'm glad for your sake.'

She shot him a charming smile; it was most encouraging.

'You know, I can't think why you want to have anything to do with him. I mean, hang it ...'

How could be explain?

'A priest's different,' he managed.

'Yes, of course.'

'He can't marry you.'

'No.'

'I've got large estates and scores of slaves.'

She watched him closely.

'So I've heard.'

'And a large mansion on the main estate and a house in the capital, of course.'

She smiled and said, 'You are very fortunate, Coatl.'

She was thinking, 'It's clear he's trying his hardest to win me. It's delicious, but why all the haste? That's the trouble with men − always in a hurry and then they tired of one so quickly. Let him keep on guessing for a bit longer.'

He plunged on clumsily, 'I mean, the woman I marry will be rich, with scores of servants. She'll have everything she wants and be one of the highest in the land. It's a darn site better than anything he can offer.'

She thought, 'I rather think he's lonely since his wife died.'

'More than that, I wouldn't go chasing other women or boys. Those days are over for me. I'd stick to her.'

'That's what he says,' she thought. But the smile she gave him was like the sun rising in springtime.

His hopes soared; but she said nothing. That was the trouble with women: you never knew what they were thinking.

He was about to go over to her and take her hands in his, when Jasmine re-entered the room. Bother!

'There's a messenger come, Mistress Lady.'

'Send him in.'

The man entered shyly, awkwardly.

'What is it?'

'A message for the Lord Jaguar Prince, my lady.'

'Who from?' Coatl asked.

'His Honour, Wise Lord Prince.'

From him!

'What does he say?'

'He requests that you, my Lord Prince, attend him at his house in the capital.'

Drat! But what else could he do? Besides, it must be important.

'Tell the Wise Lord Prince that I will come immediately.'

When they were alone again, he said, 'Darling Jewel, I fear I can't stay with you any longer.'

25

Rivalry and High Politics

It was a meeting of all the councillors and commanders. They were upset, enraged, alarmed, nearly speechless with horror and dismay.

'What has the god done to the Emperor?'

The Prince saw the High Priest dart him a look of hate. He advised attacking the strangers instantly. But the High Priest spoke strongly against it. The Emperor would only protect the god. 'He's trying to do me out of the glory,' thought the Prince sullenly. 'The hot-headed fool will land us all up in trouble,' was the High Priest's opinion.

When asked outright if he believed the stranger to be a god, the High Priest replied diplomatically, 'If he is, he will make it clear; if he is not, that, likewise, will be made clear.'

Since the Emperor believed him to be one, a flat denial would not be politic.

However greedy he might be for power, Wise Lord sensed that the time was not yet ripe. He spoke in favour of freeing Montezuma from the god's influence and of making him the real Emperor again. The High Priest felt that it would be useless to try. But he did not openly state that a new Emperor was needed – not yet. The war leaders were for immediate action, the priests against it; the other councillors wavered uncertainly.

The meeting broke up; no decision had been reached.

*　*　*　*　*　*

Hot on the heels of this came the news that the god and most of his men had left the city. Now was their chance!

The Jaguar Prince urged with might and main that they attack the remaining few instantly. Falling Eagle took his side. But Wise Lord advised caution.

'Perhaps he has gone away for good. Suppose the Emperor were harmed during the attack. The people are not yet ready to fight.'

Again, no decision was reached.

26

The Crumbling Continues

Blood dripped from the long, jagged flint knife. It splashed the High Priest's white robes and bespattered the shell-fanged, two-headed serpent mask of turquoise mosaic that he wore. Blood streamed down the altar. He killed relentlessly, with ruthless efficiency. His priests were chopping off heads and skewering them onto skull racks, then kicking the headless bodies, spurting, pouring blood, down the pyramid steps.

The worshippers were watching with gruesome, ghoulish glee, their gloating excitement rising to fever pitch. Then the Children of the Sun appeared, and spun in their circle, wheeled in their death dance. The sight of their blood drove the crowd into a frenzy. 'The sun-god! The sun-god! The sun-god!' they howled hysterically.

As they gazed enslaved and fascinated, the strangers, hearing a rumour that they would be attacked after the festival, rushed into the square and fell upon the unsuspecting people. A carnage followed. Sharp steel swords stabbed and slashed. Severed heads and legs flew through the air. Men tripped over their entrails to escape. Then the strangers withdrew to their palace.

The news spread through the city like a wind-fanned fire. The people rallied and their bloodlust turned to fury. Storming through the streets and along the canals in a screaming mob, they attacked the palace, hurling spears, arrows and rocks.

Suddenly, the Emperor himself appeared on the balcony.

There was an awed hush, a stunned silence. Taken aback,

they stood, not daring to move or even to look at him. He ordered them to cease the attack. They had nothing to fear. Calmed, quietened, quelled, they obeyed. The attack came to an end. They drifted home.

But beneath the still surface, distrust and unrest brooded. The people's faith in Montezuma was destroyed. They no longer wanted him as their ruler.

Shortly afterwards, the council elected Wise Lord as Emperor.

27

The Situation Worsens

Outrages were endless.

The councillors learned with fury that while the people had been watching the festival, the strangers had burst into the temple, knocked over the idols, prized off their gold masks and grabbed their jewels. Then they had turned on the priests and their assistants and killed them.

Next came more direful news. The god was on his way back to the city, having defeated his enemies, some of his own people, and persuaded them to join his side. Surely he *must* be a god.

An anxious council meeting was held. It was agreed to let the strangers into the city and then attack them.

An army three times larger than before marched in over the causeway and took up residence in their palace. The people watched in hostile, sullen silence.

In council, Wise Lord was adamant: 'Attack and kill every one of them.'

But the commanders quarrelled and no plan of action was drawn up.

While they were arguing, the news came. The mob had attacked the palace once more.

28

The Fury of the People

The people had risen in revolt. Hastening to the scene, the Prince saw for himself. Gathered in a shrieking, yelling mob, they were shooting arrows and flinging rocks and javelins at the mighty stone edifice.

As before, Montezuma himself suddenly appeared on the high balcony. He was wearing his most splendid robes. At the impressive sight the people hesitated, their uproar stilled. He began telling them to call off the attack. But this time their fury was uncontrollable, unquenchable. They shouted back at him that they had a new Emperor, that they would kill the strangers.

Arrows and spears began to fly once more. Some rocks struck Montezuma on the head. He withdrew, wounded. They saw him no more.

But the stone walls proved too strong. The attack was beaten off.

As the council struggled day after day to reach agreement, the news reached them that Montezuma was dead.

* * * * * *

The night was nearly moonless; it was raining heavily. The city slept in silence. Then the clattering of horses' hooves and the tramp of men's marching were heard. The strangers were breaking out of the city.

The Emperor was awakened. He ordered an immediate attack.

'They cannot escape. The drawbridges in the causeway have been taken up.'

But the enemy had made a pontoon, which they laid across the first gap and were already crossing by it.

The enraged people took to their canoes, a hundred trumpets sounded, and in the misty half-light the attack began. The fighting was savage. A shower of spears and arrows, clubs and rocks, rained like hailstones on the soldiers, who were strung out along the causeway. Many were killed, others were drowned.

Fighting desperately, doggedly, one third of them battled to the mainland and escaped. Then the pontoon bridge was broken. The rest were trapped. Some were killed. Others were made prisoner – to be dragged away and sacrificed.

29

War

The council were agreed at last: they must give battle.

But dissention followed over who was to be in command. Some wanted the Jaguar Prince kept in the capital in case it was endangered. But the High Priest pressed for his leading the army, stressing that he had the most experience. It would keep him away from her, he thought, and if he were killed, then so much the better. The Prince himself was overjoyed at the prospect; now was his chance to show them. Falling Eagle sulked: *he* should be chosen. Finally, Wise Lord, his crooked left arm wedged against his knee, settled it by appointing the Jaguar Prince.

He took an immense force with him. They paddled their way cross the lake to intercept the enemy. At Utumba the Aztec horde faced the god's small army and their Tlaxcalan allies. Victory seemed certain. But their stone-headed spears and arrows and flint-edged wooden swords were little use against cotton-padded armour and no match for steel swords and lances.

The enemy also had bows that shot heavy bolts from afar and long tubes that fired pellets like red-hot stones with a loud, frightening bang. More dangerous, they still had the volcano with them. It erupted with a terrifying flash and a roar, to send huge lumps of lava that cut down men in swaths. But worst of all were their monsters. These carried men armed with long lances and charged time and again at them. None could withstand them.

In vain, the Jaguar Prince shouted to his men to forget about taking prisoners and capture their volcano. No one heeded him. Taking prisoners was what mattered. In vain, he told them that the monsters were nothing to fear. Kill the men on their backs and they would become harmless. But his soldiers remained terrified at the sight of them and unnerved by the noise. They fought bravely while he was alive. But in the midst of a savage struggle he was struck down. His solders' hearts then failed them and they gave up the fight.

30

Opportunity – But –

The High Priest heard of the disaster. But he also learned, with ill-masked joy, that the Prince had been killed. His rival was dead! Now he was out of the way, what was there to prevent his having her? She would grieve at first, no doubt, but surely in time, would forget him. He must go to comfort and console her.

He wasted no time. But great was his astonishment and dismay to find her standing by her litter as if setting out on a journey.

'What are you doing, Jewel? You can't go now I've come.'

Momentarily taken aback, she half-hesitated, then replied in her composed fashion, 'I go to find my brother, to see if he is alive.'

Her brother, but it was the Jaguar Prince really, he knew.

'Your brother ... He was in the battle. You have no news of him?'

'No, I regret I cannot stay to welcome you.'

'Let me accompany you then.'

'There is no need, Your Excellency,' and, throwing a feathered cloak around her delicate shoulders, she stepped onto the litter. 'Fare you well,' she muttered under her breath. 'To Utumba,' she ordered the bearers, 'as fast as you can.'

They were gone and he was left alone.

* * * * * *

Her thoughts raced, as relentlessly, she urged them to hurry.

'Two armed servants should be enough. Luckily Utumba is not far distant. Dreadful ... defeat ... worse, my darling Coatl ... killed they say ... But no one seems quite sure. Perhaps ... I hope.'

The battlefield was a horrible sight. Terribly wounded men crawled about, dying of thirst, and the dead were strewn in heaps. The cries of those who had lost loved ones filled the air. The stench of blood and smoke lay pall-like over the shambles.

'Where did your commander fall?' she asked briefly.

'Here, lady,' said a soldier.

'Find him.'

'But ...'

She flourished a quill of gold dust.

'This is for the man who does so.'

31

True Love

They pulled the corpses aside without further question.

His body lay near the bottom of the heap. They dragged him free and laid him flat. She knelt beside him.

'Coatl, darling.' She put a hand on him. There was the faintest stir. 'Oh! Look! He's breathing! He's alive!' An eyelid flickered. 'He's all right.'

The men almost cheered.

'The commander's still alive. Wish we'd known.'

She nearly cried with joy.

'I'm taking him home with me. I'm going to make him well again.'

* * * * * *

Invited into the house by her head servant, the High Priest sat mulling things over complaisantly. She would soon find out that he was dead and return sorrowing, to find him here awaiting her. He would not blame her for rushing off like that. No, he would pretend to share her grief, be consoling, comfort her and, in time, win her heart. She would be lonely without the Prince and glad of her admirer ... in time, to become her lover.

* * * * * *

The servant had run all the way to bring the message.

'The Jaguar Prince is alive, though hurt, and my lady's bringing him home with her. They are on their way.'

He heard it all. So that was it! She loved the Prince. There was nothing else for it. He must go.

He made his way back, bitterly chagrined. Then rage seized him and he cursed the Jaguar Prince. Perhaps, after all, he would die, as men often did when wounded. He hoped so. As for her ... his lust turned to seething, frustrated fury. Yes, he despised and hated her too.

32

Disaster

He sulked and raged in thwarted lust for a while. Then his feelings towards her hardened. Hatred and contempt became uppermost. He would put her, both of them, out of his mind. Finally, he sought consolation with Sunshine Boy, who was a sly, grasping young acolyte.

The enemy had retreated after the mauling received at Utumba. The city seemed safe.

The summer festival went well. There were ample victims to gratify the crowd and satisfy the gods. But one thing baffled and riled the High Priest: the strangers showed neither acceptance nor fear when sacrificed. Instead, the expressions on their pale, hairy faces showed only disgust and contempt. They died bravely, calling on their invisible god for vengeance. The circling dance and stabbing of the Children of the Sun aroused the worshippers' bloodlust to a pitch of frenzy once again. Afterwards, he and his priests ate the customary meal of human flesh stewed with squash flowers. The leading commanders joined them and Wise Lord graced them with his presence.

Then suddenly a fresh disaster struck. It was sinister, evil, lethal: a disease unknown to them. A black slave had been left in the city by the enemy. One day, he broke out in pitted spots and ran a high fever. A few days later he died. Then one of their own people perished in the same way, then more and more of them. They died like flies. No medicines could cure, nothing could stay its progress. The plague spread through the city like a raging fire. But the accused strangers, who had brought it to them, seldom died of it themselves. Then worse befell. Wise Lord caught it. He died a few days later. The councillors elected Falling Eagle as Emperor. He was their bravest commander – but he was young and untried.

33

Jewel and Coatl

'I owe my life to you, my darling, Jewel,' he said.

They were sitting outside; the evening had brought a pleasant coolness.

'I'm so glad you are well once more, my dear Coatl.'

She smiled and, as he looked at her fondly, he thought of her bent over him as she tended him by day and night. His love for her had deepened. She knew now that her real love was for him. How could she have shilly-shallied for so long? She was overjoyed that he was with her and that he loved her so much. Pochtli was now but a distasteful, fading memory.

He embraced and kissed her fondly and she warmed to him. They kissed passionately. What paradise!

They watched the stars coming out in silver pinpoints and the moon, slowly, mistily rising. How wonderful to be together. How could she ever have doubted him?

A few days later, they were sitting talking in the cool, inner room. Outside the land baked in ferocious summer hear.

He was looking sombre and thoughtful.

'What's on his mind?' she asked herself.

At last he spoke.

'The enemy are preparing for another battle.'

'Are they? How do you know?'

'I make it my business to keep in touch with these things.'

She was concerned.

He went on, 'They have got more of that white powder that makes their volcano go with a bang and throw lava at us and they are building their big canoes with the huge cloths that make the wind drive them along.'

'Oh! Why?'

'So that they can cross the Moon Lake and attack the capital.'

'Oh! No! How dreadful. But, you won't go there, will you?'

'I'll see.'

She watched him closely. As his strength returned he became more and more restless and preoccupied.

One day, he said, 'I must go to the city. I must advise them on what they're to do.'

She was alarmed.

'But Coatl, darling, it's not safe. You haven't heard. There's a terrible plague there. You'd die of it. Please don't go near.'

'I had heard.'

'And you know that Falling Eagle is Emperor now and he won't listen to you and Pochtli will turn him and everyone against you. So what's the use? You wouldn't be doing any good at all. Please stay with me. I'm afraid of being left on my own, in case he comes.'

'Are you really, darling?'

'Yes, I am.'

A struggle went on in his mind.

'All right then.' He relented, at last, with a smile. 'I'll stay and keep you safe.'

34

Danger

Fear and uncertainty had been hanging over the city like a black storm cloud; the return of the defeated soldiers upset people further. Preparations for war were feverish, hasty. Then scouts brought information that the enemy was breaking camp.

Falling Eagle called on the nearest tributary tribes for help. A vast army of them poured into the city but they were of doubtful loyalty. Each war chief kept command of his own people, quarrels were endless and agreeing on a plan of campaign proved impossible. The young Emperor was nearly desperate. Then they learned that the enemy was approaching. The city was thrown into turmoil.

* * * * * *

The High Priest had planned ahead and the victims had been brought to the city ready for the vital pre-harvest sacrifices. The Children of the Sun, large numbers of them, were ensconced in the temple buildings.

After that he had time to think. It gave him pain upon pain. He had tired of Sunshine Boy and his thoughts were full of her once more. 'Jewel, did you ever love me at all, or was it always him?' The Prince was with her all the time now. What were they doing, saying to each other? Now he was desperate, sleepless with mental torment. He would get him away from her. He would persuade Falling Eagle to recall him. With danger threatening, the Prince was needed in the capital. But he must be diplomatic; the new Emperor disliked the man.

*   *   *   *   *   *

The all-important audience was the next day. But the High Priest was overwrought with anxiety. He must first have a good night's sleep. Yes, there was some liquid left in the tiny jug ...

For a second he hesitated, remembering what had happened the last time. But he was desperate – he must have it. Ah! What relief ... what restfulness. Peace of mind filled him, at last he was at ease. Thoughts pleasant floated into his mind ... troubles were swept, soothed, smoothed away. He could laugh at them now. They were unreal, forgotten. Now he was drifting slowly upwards, borne aloft into the air ... wafting about ... being blown gently to and fro like floating seeds ... then carried up into the sky ... warm, soft, light, weightless. He was floating out into space, slowly, easily ... further and further ... swept into the heavens themselves ... where the mighty god, the sun, blazed forth fiery, fierce. The stars drew near, brilliant, sparkling light points. He was being carried further, caught up ... drawn towards the sun, to turn slowly around ... the glorious, radiant shining orb. He was irresistibly spinning round him in eddies ... circling in a rush ... whirling round faster and faster. He was being drawn closer to the mighty deity, the effulgent fiery, glowing god ... who was now sucking him like a whirlpool nearer and nearer ... to himself ... to swallow him ... a fiery consummation that would destroy him.

Horror struck him! Dread terror! He tried to scream, even as the sacrificial victims screamed in their death throes, but no sound came. He fought, struggled, writhed in agony ... but he could not move. He was helpless. No! ... Not this! Destruction glared at him ... black nothingness ... annihilation ... death.

He awoke, feeling misty, hazy, dry, thick and torpid. It was already noon. He struggled to rise and start the journey. But before he could reach the palace he learnt that the enemy was marching on the city. The Emperor was attending a council of war.

He was too late.

35

The City Besieged

The attack was coming. Divided into three columns, the enemy approached the causeways. Crowds of Tlaxcalans helped to launch their huge canoes. Well-armed soldiers embarked on them, and one carried the volcano. Another force smashed the aqueduct that brought fresh water to the city. Now its inhabitants must depend on wells and lake water.

Fighting broke out at dawn one day; the enemy gained a foothold on the causeways. The defenders attacked them with hails of spears and arrows, clubs and rocks. Soldiers crowded the causeways; warriors crammed the war canoes. The sound of guns firing, trumpets blowing, men shouting and the wounded screaming made a ceaseless deafening din.

At first, they held the enemy back as they struggled to force their way forward. But then, at a command from their god-leader, the men with the long tubes would fire their rock pellets with a hideous bang and the foremost warriors fell like stalks of maize before a storm. Then there was the volcano. Travelling on one of their swift moving, wind-blown canoes, it would come to where the fighting was thickest, the resistance most stubborn. A flash and a loud bang and the lumps of lava flew through the air, cutting a pathway through the densely packed defenders. Their wooden, feather-decorated shields and plumed helmets gave no protection. The instant that they gave way, the enemy pressed forward a few paces.

Day after day the savage struggle went on and always the enemy advanced nearer the city.

36

She is Crafty and Wise

'Who is it for?' she asked.

'The Jaguar Prince, O Precious Jewel Lady,' replied the man smoothly.

'The Prince is resting. What is your message?' He hesitated. 'You may tell it to me.'

'His Imperial Majesty, the Emperor, orders the Prince to return to the capital without delay.'

'Oh!' Although taken aback and alarmed, something within her said, 'This does not sound as if it comes from Falling Eagle at all.' 'Really!' she managed. 'Did the Emperor himself tell you to say this?' She studied the messenger closely – no, there was something about him that was ... different. 'I do not believe it comes from him.' The man remained silent, yet composed. 'Tell me who really sent it and I will make it worth your while,' and she touched her gold bracelet.

She saw his eyes flicker and after much hesitation, he replied, 'His Excellency, the High Priest, sent me with it.'

She was dumbfounded. Her eyes opened wide.

'I see.' Pochtli! From him! By one of his temple servants, of course; that explained it. She said, 'Very well. I will tell the Prince that you have a message for him. What is happening in the city?'

'The enemy are making some advances, but not much,' was the suave reply.

She dismissed him with, 'I see. You may rest here before you return.'

Alone, her thoughts teemed through her mind like rain pouring on the roof. 'A trick of his ... to get Coatl away from me, of course. How cunning. He might have believed it and gone. It's still possible to cross the lake, then there'd be nothing to stop Pochtli coming here and finding me alone. Ugh!'

'Tell my Lord Prince what you have just told me.' She touched her bracelet; the man's eyes followed her movement.

'Curious, a command of this kind coming from the High Priest. Are you sure?'

'Quite sure, my Lord Prince.'

'I see. I will think what answer to give him.'

The messenger withdrew.

Coatl said, 'He may be the High Priest, but he's got a nerve giving orders like that. If the Emperor came to hear of it ...'

'Yes dear. How right you are.' She paused. 'Under the circumstances, it would be better for you not to return to the capital. If you did, it would look like defiance of His Imperial Majesty's wishes.'

He gave her a straight look.

'Yes, it would.' After chewing it over thoughtfully, he said, 'I'll send a message to your brother instead of going. He'll know how to suggest it to the Emperor tactfully.'

The messenger listened patiently as the Prince said, 'To your master, the High Priest, I have nothing to say. But I want this given to Green Jade Lord. It is this: "Sink the canoe with their volcano at all costs." Right! Go as soon as you can.'

'This is for your trouble,' she said, 'and I know Green Jade Lord will reward you, too.'

A glitter of grateful greed came into the man's eyes. He bowed and left. He was wearing the gold bracelet.

*　*　*　*　*　*

The messenger picked his way warily to the lake edge. The canoe was there ... good ... better wait until dusk and go across under cover of darkness. But the lake looked clear of craft and there was a rich reward awaiting him.

He paddled out from shore cautiously, furtively, looking around him. Nothing in sight ... but halfway across ... what was this coming? One of the enemy canoes was bearing down on him, moving swiftly, faster than men could drive it. No matter how hard he paddled, it drew nearer. It was gliding towards him like a bird flying. It was close. A soldier in it was fitting something long and hard into a strange thing he held across his knee. He raised and pointed it. Something hard and heavy flew through the air. It struck him on the head. He was killed instantly.

* * * * * *

'It was quick of you to see through his trick,' Coatl said.

Her eyes twinkled and she smiled charmingly.

'I had my suspicions he was up to no good.'

'He gazed at her longingly.

'I'm so glad to be here with you, Jewel.'

'So am I and it's wonderful to know you're better again, Coatl, darling.'

'It certainly is and, what's more, I think you've gone off him too.'

She gave him a look.

'Yes, I have, completely.'

They both laughed and, smiling triumphantly, he said, 'You are ready to say "yes" at last.'

'Yes, I am, Coatl and I'm sure my brother will agree.'

They embraced each other and kissed with growing feeling. She gave him an arch look.

'Think of tonight, darling.'

'Darling, Jewel, you have made me happy.'

'Darling, Coatl, you have made me happy too. I'll get the marriage-maker to come, shall I, and fix the day?'

'The sooner, the better.'

37

Defeat

Stubbornly the foe advanced. The defenders lacked their weapons of steel and fire, and their determination to kill. Intent on taking prisoners, they tried to capture their enemies alive. Grabbing these, they dragged them off, screaming tribesmen and doggedly silent strangers alike. The altar ran blood like a river. The gods of war were satiated; the sun shone in flaming heat and brilliance. But it took up men needed for fighting. The hideous clamour of firing, clashing of weapons, shouting and screaming was ceaseless, wearing.

Day after day the enemy pressed nearer to the city.

Diseases began to ravage the defenders as they drank impure water. The supply of weapons ran short. The undisciplined warriors fought as they chose; the war chiefs quarrelled; desertion became wholesale.

Still the enemy drew nearer. They made a footing on the last section of the causeway. Their flashes of lightning were close and the thatched roofs of the nearby huts caught alight. Red flames rose high, sparks flew. From roof to roof they leapt and the city was on fire.

The defence crumbled. The enemy forced its way into the capital itself. Beaten, the warriors took to their canoes and fled across the lake.

Falling Eagle sued for peace.

* * * * * *

In a silence so sudden and complete that men wondered if they had gone deaf, the Emperor resentfully surrendered the city to its conqueror.

38

Collapse

The High Priest was alone in his cell in the temple buildings. Beyond, the city was still burning, its people in flight. The conquerors marched through it as they chose, grabbing any gold that they could find and torturing the people to make them tell where they had any hidden. They had knocked down the idols in the temple and killed the priests who tried to stop them. Rumours first said that the Emperor had escaped, but then, that he was a prisoner of the strangers. The hated Tlaxcalans were insolently triumphant. The citizens who remained lived in terror.

Was this the revenge of the rejected god of wind and life?

His mind went back to an audience with the god and how his own arrogant assertions had met with a harsh indifference, an adamant conviction, that rejected all he believed. The god ruled now. Their religion would be swept away, their vital sacrifices forbidden.

But a worse loss stabbed his heart. His Precious Jewel ... he had lost her ... and to that blockhead of a soldier. They were married now. The thought tore him to pieces. 'Jewel,' he cried in torment, 'I want you so much. You deceived me. All the while it was him you loved.' There was no chance of winning her back. Those two were happy together, while he was cast out. It twisted him to think of it. He burned in an agony of jealousy, a fury of grief and resentment. He longed to kill them both ... sacrifice them. 'If I can't have her, why should he?'

But he was powerless to do anything but burn in helpless

self-torture. There was no one to help him. Men had hated and feared him; now they feared him no longer. He had no friends. His importance and power were gone. He had nothing left to live for; he wanted only to die.

The priest medicine man handed him the potion.

'This liquid will ensure a quick, painless end, Your Excellency.'

Did he see an evil glint in the fellow's eye, as he spoke? But he was past caring.

He drank it and lay on his couch. Now for a swift, easy end to it all. But no! Something gripped him, first a cramping of the stomach, then pain ... sharper pain. The ripping caught at his entrails, twisting, convulsing him. He was corrugated by it. In agonies he writhed, sweating, biting his tongue, screaming ... Too late, now, he realised that the miserable fellow had cheated him again. His wretched medicine had made him miss the vital audiences with the Emperor, when he might have saved their land from disaster, and for days afterwards a woman was of no use to him. Now the same fellow had condemned him to an agonising death.

Outside, the Children of the Sun played in the sunlit courtyard. The sound of their heedless laughing and singing floated to his ears as he lay in his tormented death throes.

A sudden commotion.

'Who are these?' the conqueror god demanded.

'The victims for the next sacrifice, Your Honour.'

A look of pity flashed across the stern face, followed by one of disgusted disapproval.

'Let them go!' Cortés snapped.

'But, Your Honour ...'

'Let them go immediately! Tell them that they are free to do so. The One True God wants no victims. He hates human sacrifice. He has accepted the sacrifice of His Blessed Son, Our Saviour, as sufficient – thanks be to the Blessed Mary, His Mother.'

They hesitated. Cortés drew his sword. When the priests tried to prevent the children leaving, the soldiers drove them off with their pikes. Priests who resisted were slain. The acolytes were herded back. A sword was held at the throat of the priest who had led them in the obscene sacrificial dances. The temple guards were killed; the gates flung wide open.

For the High Priest, life itself was ebbing away. Death faced him. Darkness was coming down, closing in on him ... the darkness of death.

Bewildered at first, the children watched uncomprehending as, one by one, the chains that had held them captive were broken.

Still the god urged them resolutely to leave their prison house and still they stood there, uncertain.

Then understanding came. Nothing was left to hold them there, to enslave them for a hideous death. Realisation, relief, went through them, like a gust of fresh wind, wafting through waving maize.

Laughing and dancing, they moved towards the entrance. Then they ran tripping, skipping past the grim, thick, imprisoning walls, beneath the high stone archway and past the heavy gates. Out through them and into the burning city they scampered unhindered, joyfully, and as they went they sang –

'We are the Children of the sun-god, children of the sun-god, Children of the sun.'